Decisions of the Heart

RAMONE

Copyright © 2024 Ramone
All rights reserved
First Edition

NEWMAN SPRINGS PUBLISHING
320 Broad Street
Red Bank, NJ 07701

First originally published by Newman
Springs Publishing 2024

This novel is fiction. All the characters are
purely fictional in the making of this novel.

ISBN 979-8-89061-700-2 (Paperback)
ISBN 979-8-89061-701-9 (Digital)

Printed in the United States of America

CHAPTER 1

ONE BRIGHT, SUNNY MORNING, A YOUNG LADY gets in her SUV. As soon as she starts the truck, one of her favorite songs comes on. The name of the song is "I Do Love You" by GQ. As she drives to work, she bops her head as if she really enjoys the music. She puts her shades on for a cooler look, or maybe to block the sun out, or maybe both. Then she drives to work while bopping her head to the music.

Jennifer Day is a White female, thirty. Joann Wells is a White female, thirty-five. Bob is a White male, thirty-five. Johnny is a Black male, thirty-five.

She works in an office building. She is strictly professional. She wears dress suits every day to work. When she's not working, she wears casual jeans. Her name is Jennifer Day. As she goes to work and enters the building, she smiles and says hello to all her coworkers. They all smile and say hello back. She makes it to her desk, which is surrounded by other desks with wall stands about six feet tall. While sipping her coffee, her friend and coworker, whose name is Joann Wells, asks her, "So how did it go last night?"

She then answers in Spanish, "Nada." Jennifer continues, "I believe there's something going on."

Joann says, "Why say something like that when you are not sure about it?"

Jennifer replies, "Well, last night, I told my boyfriend, Charles, that we need some quality time together. But whenever he comes home, he's too tired to do anything."

Then Joann replies, "But he's working a second job, right?"

Jennifer replies, "I know he's working really hard. I know that."

Joann says, "And you told me he said he's working really hard for the both of you, right?"

Jennifer says, "Why are you making me look like I'm the bad guy?"

There are two other coworkers listening to the conversation between Jennifer and Joann. One of the men's name is Bob. Bob's comment to Jennifer is, "Maybe you should start taking cold showers like we do."

Jennifer replies, "Bite me."

DECISIONS OF THE HEART

Bob starts laughing. The other man, whose name is Johnny, says to Jennifer, "Jennifer, don't listen to him. He's not as smart as he looks."

Bob replies, "Thank you," in a well-mannered way.

Johnny says, "You're welcome," in the same manner.

So Jennifer turns to Joann and says, "So you think I'm blowing this thing out of proportion?"

Joann replies, "Yes, way out of proportion. Don't make a mountain out of a rock."

Jennifer replies, "So even though we haven't had sex for two months, and he kisses me on the cheeks and not the lips, and we are always arguing about the stupidest things that don't make any kind of sense, and you think I'm being paranoid?"

Joann replies, "Yes! Stop complaining and just start showing support."

Jennifer replies, "You're right. Maybe I am just thinking of myself a little bit."

Joann says, "*A little bit* is not the word."

Jennifer says in a mild manner, "Yeah, yeah, yeah." Then Jennifer and Joann turn to the guys. Jennifer says, "So which one of you guys is paying for lunch?" The guys look at each other and hide behind the walls, and Bob says Johnny is, and Johnny says Bob is, and they both say it at the same time.

Jennifer and Joann look at each other, and Joann says, "If we were dating these guys, we would be in big trouble." Jennifer nods her head in a yes manner. The day is over, everyone says goodbye, and Jennifer heads to her car.

Jennifer drives home, pulls over in front of her apartment building, and walks up the stairs. She checks her mail and goes in. As she enters, she hears her boyfriend Charles talking on the phone, very softly. She enters the room where Charles is, and he says, "I got to go," and then he hangs up.

Jennifer asks him, "Who are you talking to?"

Charles replies, "My brother."

Jennifer says, "Since when did you start talking to your brother so softly? Did they make a big improvement on his hearing aid?"

Charles yells, "Hey! Stop asking me all these gotdamn questions." Then he storms out of the apartment and slams the door so hard it shakes the windows and Jennifer too. She puts both hands on the kitchen chair and starts crying silently.

She says to herself, "What is going on? God, please help me!"

DECISIONS OF THE HEART

Jennifer waits for Charles to come home. She is in the front room, watching TV, curled up on the couch in her short nighty which comes above her knees, hoping she can make up with Charles.

It's 3:30 a.m. Charles comes through the door and looks at her and says, "What is it now?"

Jennifer replies, "I was waiting for you. I wanted to apologize for what happened today." She stands up, looking very sexy in her see-through nighty, and says, "Will you forgive me?"

Charles replies, "Yes," and then he heads for bed.

Jennifer stands in the living room, puzzled because Charles ignored her in her sexy nighty. So she calmly walks into the bedroom where Charles is lying peacefully. She lies by his side with her head on his chest, stroking his stomach with her soft hands.

He grabs her hands and says, "Not tonight. I'm tired, okay?"

Jennifer is devastated. She can't understand why he is so tired when he didn't even go to work that day and why he is totally ignoring her in her sexy nighty. Then she notices a Band-Aid on his neck. She asks, "What happened to your neck?"

He replies, "I was stung by a bee or something."

Jennifer says, "Did you put something on it?"

Charles says, "Yes, don't worry about it. Just go to sleep." Then he turns over on his right side to go to sleep. Jennifer lies back, looks up at the ceiling, then turns her head to her left side, and finds herself looking in the mirror. She notices something and becomes very nervous. She can see Charles's back reflecting in the mirror, and there are fresh scratches on his back. So she gets up out of bed with a look on her face as if she has seen a ghost. She goes to another room, sits in a corner, holds her stomach, and begins to cry softly.

CHAPTER 2

The next day at work, Jennifer sits at her desk very quietly. Her friend Joann says, "What's wrong?"

Jennifer shakes her head and says, "Nothing."

Then Bob says, "Maybe she's tired of those cold showers," and then he laughs.

Jennifer puts her head down and starts to cry. Johnny turns to Bob and says, "Are you happy now?"

Bob replies, "I was just joking," and then he apologizes to Jennifer.

Joann holds Jennifer in her arms to comfort her. Joann asks again, "Please tell me what's wrong. I'm your friend. I love you."

So Jennifer tells her what happened last night, about the scratches on Charles's back and the Band-Aid on his neck, and how he simply ignored her. Joann replies, "Maybe he fell and scratched his back or something."

Jennifer replies, "These scratches don't look accidental. They look intentional, and he didn't want me to touch him. I lay practically naked with him in bed, and he didn't even look at me."

Joann replies, "Maybe you're being paranoid again."

Before Joann could finish the whole sentence, Jennifer yells, "Don't tell me I'm being paranoid. I know what I saw, I know what I felt inside my heart, and I don't know why in God's name you are protecting him!"

"I am not protecting him. I am just trying to make you see that you could be wrong about him!"

Johnny and Bob cut into the heated discussion that Jennifer and Joann are having and say, "Guys, can we finish this conversation at lunch before everyone in the office hears about this?"

So Jennifer and Joann calm down a little. Jennifer says, "I think he's fooling around with me."

Joann says, "Don't say that. Charles loves you."

Jennifer replies, "If you told me that two months ago, I would have believed you." While sitting at her desk, she holds her head up with her left hand as if she had a migraine headache.

Joann says, "You know what?"

DECISIONS OF THE HEART

Jennifer replies, "No, I don't, and as a matter of fact, I don't know anything anymore."

Joann says, "I bet when you get home, Charles is going to be waiting for you with open arms."

Jennifer replies, "Yeah right, and I am Julia Roberts!"

Joann replies, "Well, we will see what happens tomorrow."

Joann says, "Oh, I got to make a call, and I left my cell phone in the car."

Jennifer replies, "Oh, you can use my phone."

Joann says, "I don't trust these office phones. They might be listening. I'll go use my phone I always use in the front entrance. I'll be right back."

Jennifer starts doing her work. Bob asks her, "Are you alright?"

Jennifer says, "Yes, thank you."

Johnny then says, "Do you want us to go and give Charles a beat down? Just let us know!"

Jennifer laughs and says, "No. Thank you guys for being here for me. I'll be alright."

CHAPTER 3

AFTER WORK, JENNIFER GETS INTO HER CAR and puts in a CD titled "Good to Go" by Lugo. Jennifer drives home and pulls in front of her apartment. She walks upstairs, checks her mailbox, and enters the apartment.

She walks into the bedroom, and Charles is waiting. She says, "What's going on?" Charles, wearing an unbuttoned shirt, blue jeans, and white sneakers, walks up to Jennifer and lays her down, raising her skirt. He unzips his pants; he is wearing boxer shorts, so it is easy to access. Jennifer says to Charles, "Can we take our clothes off first?" Charles ignores her wishes and continues to have sex with her very rapidly.

Three to five minutes later, it is over. Charles gets up, goes to the bathroom, and says to her, "Are you satisfied now?"

Jennifer waits until he leaves the room and says to herself, "No, no, I'm not."

Still lying there in bed with all her clothes on, she begins to cry softly. Charles comes back into the bedroom with a different set of clothes and cologne. Jennifer says to Charles, "What's going on with you?"

Charles replies, "What the fuck is your problem? You complain about needing to spend quality time together, and we did. You complain about not having sex anymore, and we just did! What the fuck do you want from me?"

Jennifer replies, "I'll tell you what I want from you: love, respect, and honor! That's what I'm giving you, and that's what I want in return."

Charles replies, "I have given you that. You just can't be satisfied or content, no matter what I do for your ungrateful ass."

Jennifer replies, "You have the nerve to call me ungrateful."

Charles replies, "You're damn right."

Jennifer replies, "You come in at 3:00 a.m. and then cry about how tired you are, even on a day you didn't even go to work."

In the background, Charles repeats, "Yeah, bitch, whatever."

RAMONE

Jennifer then says, "You have a Band-Aid on your neck, which is probably a hickey, and you have scratches on your back that you don't bother to explain to me! And that's because you can't explain what some bitch out there did to your back and neck. Because you're too fucking chicken to just come out and tell me the fucking truth! And then you call yourself having sex with me? Two months ago, you called it making love to me! I guess that's when you started fucking around with Ms. Bitch. Then you come bringing your no-good, nasty, fuck-anything-that-moves ass home to me!"

Charles, in the background, says, "Watch your mouth before you piss me off."

Jennifer replies, "Speaking of *off*. You lie down on me for three minutes, then spring off like a fucking yo-yo, get dressed, put on some old funky cologne—what Ms. Bitch probably bought you—and are ready to spring out the door, like you just did a job on me. I could have gotten off better with a gotdamn vibrator."

Charles becomes furious and turns to Jennifer, yelling, "Shut the fuck up."

He then slaps her so hard that Jennifer goes airborne backward and falls over the couch. Charles rushes out the front door, leaving Jennifer crying very loudly. She calls her friend Joann for comfort, but Joann doesn't answer, so Jennifer goes and takes a shower, still crying. She gets dressed and goes for a walk to think things over. As Jennifer takes her walk, she stops by the store and gets a drink. The cashier says to her, "That's a fine drink."

Jennifer replies, "It doesn't matter. After crying, your mouth gets dry." She says thank you to the cashier and leaves.

CHAPTER 4

IT'S NOW 9:30 P.M., AND IT'S DARK outside. The only lights are the streetlights and the moonlight. As Jennifer walks toward her apartment, she is about twenty feet away when a man with a mask, gloves, and a long black trench coat steps out of the shadows. Jennifer doesn't know what is about to happen, and suddenly, she is attacked from the back. The stranger covers her mouth with one hand and grabs her around her waist with the other hand. He whispers in her ear, very softly, "Don't worry. You're alright now." He carries her to an alley, while she is kicking and struggling.

He takes his hands from her mouth, and Jennifer whispers, "Please, please don't kill me. Please don't hurt me." The stranger, standing behind her and pressing her against the van, then puts her inside the van. He lies her on her stomach, puts duct tape on her mouth, and ties her hands behind her back.

DECISIONS OF THE HEART

Someone is walking past the van but doesn't notice anything unusual. The van pulls off very slowly as if nothing is going on.

CHAPTER 5

THE VAN PULLS INTO A MOTEL. THE stranger walks to the front desk and says to the hotel clerk, "I want a room." The stranger still displays his mask on his face.

The clerk asks, "What's with the mask?"

The stranger replies, "Costume party." So the clerk rents him a room. The stranger quietly carries her into the room. He lays her on the bed. Jennifer is crying the whole time.

He ties her hands to each bedpost and then ties her feet to the bottom bedpost. Jennifer is terrified; she looks up at him but cannot see his face. She can only see his eyes. She couldn't even tell what race he is. Then the stranger tells her if she is quiet, he will take the duct tape off her mouth. Jennifer nods her head, saying yes with tears in her eyes.

So the stranger removes the tape. Jennifer is breathing very rapidly. The stranger says to her, "Don't worry. You're alright because I'm here for you."

Jennifer's eye is blackened from the slap her boyfriend gave her. The stranger whispers to her, "What happened to your eye?"

Jennifer replies, "My boyfriend hit me."

The stranger says, "How could a man his size hit a woman as beautiful as you?"

She replies, "How do you know what size he is?"

The stranger replies, "I know everything. I know how he mistreats you. I know how he's fucking around on you. I know how he treats you like garbage. You deserve better than that. You should be with someone who loves you, someone who cares for you, someone who will give their life so that you could live, and someone who would appreciate you for who you are."

Jennifer looks very curious and puzzled. She wonders how he knows about her. So she asks him, "How do you know so much about me?"

The stranger replies, "Because I feel you." The stranger speaks with a very soft voice. "I feel what you feel. I hurt when you hurt. When your boyfriend hit you, I felt it."

RAMONE

Jennifer asks, "How would you feel if you were not there?"

The stranger replies, "I was there. I was there watching. I saw the argument, I saw the slap, I saw your boyfriend going to the toilet on you, and you did the right thing to go wash him off."

Jennifer asks, "Where were you while observing all this?"

The stranger replies, "I watched through the window, in the closet, and under the bed. I didn't do it out of being a freak or whatever you think. I did it because I cared about you, and I didn't like the way he treated you."

Jennifer says to the stranger, "If you care about me, why are you doing this? Why don't you let me go?"

The stranger replies, "I'm doing this because I love you, and I want you to know that we are meant to be together. We deserve each other's love."

The stranger starts taking Jennifer's clothes off very gently. Jennifer begins to say, "No, no, no! Please let me go." She's crying at the same time.

The stranger says to her, "Don't worry. You're alright." So the stranger starts caressing Jennifer's body from her head to her toes. Very slowly, he then begins oral sex on her. Jennifer is fighting the feeling with all her might. But then something happens. Jennifer can no longer hold on to something she's been holding in for the longest time; she actually gets very angry with herself. What happens next is unimaginable; Jennifer has an orgasm, but she still cries out to the stranger, "No, please stop." During this scene, a song is playing called "We Deserve Each Other's Love" by Jeffrey Osborne.

And then the stranger gets on top of Jennifer between her soft, creamy thighs and starts making love to her, telling her the whole time that he loves her, he will never leave or hurt her, and no one else will hurt her ever again.

Jennifer turns her head to her right side and closes her eyes, beginning to cry again in fear.

The next morning, Jennifer awakens still lying in bed, but there is no sign of the stranger. She's still tied to the bed, and there's a note on her stomach that says, "I finally found you, and we deserve each other's love." She struggles but can't get free.

Meanwhile, at work, her colleagues are worried. "Jennifer never came a day late in her life," Joann says to the other coworkers.

Bob and Johnny say to Joann, "Why don't you call her home and talk to Charles?"

Joann replies, "I did a hundred times already."

CHAPTER 6

At the police district, they receive a call saying there's a woman tied up in room 28 who needs help. The desk sergeant takes the call and tells the rest of the officers that he just received a crank call. The lieutenant asks, "What did they say?"

The desk sergeant says, "A woman is tied up in a hotel room."

And the lieutenant replies, "Send some units to the hotel right now!"

The lieutenant and a few units pull into the parking lot of the hotel with their siren on and their guns out. The lieutenant directs all the officers into a safe position in case it's an ambush. On the count of three, the lieutenant signals all the officers to kick the door. The door flies open, and the lieutenant discovers Jennifer tied to the bed. He covers her up with a blanket. Jennifer is screaming, "Help me, help me!" The lieutenant unties her and has an ambulance summoned, telling her he will meet her at the hospital after he asks the hotel some questions.

The lieutenant makes his way into the hotel lobby to talk to the clerk. Lt. Bronson asks, "So what happened?"

The clerk says, "I don't know what happened. All I do is rent the rooms out, and that's all."

Lt. Bronson says, "Let me see the register book." The clerk hands it to him and sits down very calmly. The lieutenant added, "He's probably registered under an alias name."

Then the clerk says, "Let me show you where he signed in." The clerk shows the lieutenant the signature.

The lieutenant looks and says, "What the hell is this?"

The clerk says, "I had no idea that is how he signed in." The signature was all scrambled, like a one-year-old signed it. The lieutenant asks the clerk to describe him. The clerk says to the lieutenant, "Well, that might be a problem." The lieutenant asks why. The clerk says, "The suspect had on a costume."

The lieutenant begins to get angry. He says, "You mean to tell me you let someone rent a room with a phony signature and a costume mask without checking him out?"

The clerk replies, "Well, I asked what's with the mask, and he said he and his girlfriend just came from a costume party. So I thought they were a couple of kids having fun."

The lieutenant gets silent, then he says, "You have to read a book to be that stupid." Then he tells the clerk, "Don't plan any trips because we are going to see what the city has to say about you renting out rooms while a crime is being committed. We will keep in touch." So the lieutenant leaves and heads for the hospital to talk to Jennifer.

When Lt. Bronson arrives at the hospital, he heads straight for the emergency room. When he gets there, the doctors are checking Jennifer out. The lieutenant asks, "Can I ask you a few questions?" Jennifer nods her head in a yes manner. The lieutenant asks, "Did he hurt you?"

Jennifer replies, "No."

The lieutenant asks, "Can you describe him?"

Jennifer says, "He had on a mask. I couldn't see anything but his eyes."

The lieutenant asks, "What color were they?"

Jennifer says, "They were brown, and that's all I saw."

DECISIONS OF THE HEART

The lieutenant asks, "Did you see any tattoos or any kind of marks on his hands or body? Anything that can help me find this guy?"

Jennifer says, "He had on gloves. I couldn't see anything. But there's one thing I can tell you." The lieutenant asks what. Jennifer says, "His voice. He spoke very softly. I will never forget it."

Then Jennifer starts to cry. Another woman approaches Lt. Bronson and introduces herself. She says, "Excuse me, Lieutenant. You are upsetting her."

The lieutenant asks, "Okay, who are you?"

The lady says, "I am Karen Gills. I am the rape advocate from the health center. And I need to talk to her, okay?"

The lieutenant replies, "I am just doing my job."

Then Karen Gills says, "Thank you, and close the door behind you when you leave."

So one of the lieutenant's officers asks, "So what do we have to go on?"

The lieutenant replies, "We have nothing. Nothing at all."

So they leave.

CHAPTER 7

Now Jennifer is at home in her sleeping wear, watching TV. Then Charles comes in and says, "Are you okay?"

Jennifer replies, "Yes, thank you."

Charles says to Jennifer, "I'm going out for a little while. I'll be back soon, okay?"

Jennifer answers, "Okay."

Time goes by and day turns into night. Charles still has not returned yet, and Jennifer hears a sound coming from her computer; she's got mail. She sits down at the computer and checks her mail.

It says, "Hi, I miss you."

Jennifer replies, "Who are you?"

The screen says, "It's me."

Jennifer begins to lose her breath, and she runs to the phone to call Lt. Bronson. When the lieutenant arrives, he asks her, "Are you okay?"

Jennifer replies, "Yes, I'm okay."

DECISIONS OF THE HEART

The lieutenant asks, "What happened?" Jennifer shows him the email message on the computer. So the lieutenant asks her to respond to the mail on the computer. She responds, but there is no answer. So the lieutenant tells his officers to check the apartment before they leave, and he tells Jennifer that if she hears or sees anything or needs to talk to him, please call, because they want to catch this guy. She says okay and thank you. The lieutenant and the officers leave, and Jennifer is all alone again. But before the lieutenant leaves, he asks Jennifer, "Who else has your email address?"

She tells him about her friends and coworkers. So Jennifer goes to question all her friends and coworkers. She calls her friend Joann for comfort. Joann answers the phone while laughing. "Hello?"

Jennifer says, "Hi, it's me."

Joann says, "How are you? Are you okay?"

Jennifer says, "I am okay. I just need someone to talk to, you know?"

Joann says, "Yes, it's okay. I was coming to see you today anyway."

Jennifer says, "That would be nice. I could use the company." Then Jennifer asks, "How's everything at work?"

RAMONE

Joann says, "Everything is okay. Everyone wants to know when you are coming back to work, especially Bob and Johnny."

Jennifer replies, "What are those two guys up to anyway?"

Joann says, "They're just saying how they want to find this guy and put his head on a platter for you."

Jennifer says, "That's nice of them." So Jennifer asks Joann, "Do you have any company right now?"

Joann replies, "Yes, my boyfriend is over." Then she says to her boyfriend, "Can you wait until I get off the phone first?"

Then Jennifer can hear the boyfriend in the background saying, "Hurry up."

And then Joann says to Jennifer, "He is so impatient."

Jennifer asks, "Is he anyone I know?"

Joann says, "No, just some guy I know." Joann says to Jennifer, "Look, I have to go, but I will be over later to see you, okay?"

Jennifer says, "Okay, I will see you later."

Joann says, "I love you." And Jennifer says the same thing. And then they both hang up.

CHAPTER 8

It's nighttime now. Jennifer is in the front room watching television. She hears a sound in the back and gets up, calling out, "Charles, is that you?" Then as she walks toward the back door very slowly, the closer she gets, the more fear she feels. She finally makes it to the back door, and there is nothing there, so she takes a deep breath and says to herself, "I must be going crazy." Suddenly, the stranger appears from out of the closet, grabs her mouth, looks her straight into her eyes, and then hands her a note, whispering to her, "Read it. She's not what you think." Then he strokes her face very softly, gently moves her hair from the front of her face, and then he leaves.

So Jennifer runs to the phone and calls Lt. Bronson, and then she calls her friend Joann. They arrive at about the same time. The lieutenant says, "What happened?"

Jennifer says, "He was here," crying at the same time. The lieutenant asks, "Did he hurt you? Did he take anything?"

Jennifer says, "No, he didn't hurt me or take anything." So Jennifer hides the note after she reads it.

The lieutenant says, "I'm going to put a unit outside for surveillance. If you see anything or hear anything, don't hesitate to tell the officers outside to contact me, okay?"

Jennifer replies, "Okay," and then he leaves.

So Joann asks Jennifer, "What happened? Tell me."

Jennifer says, "He came in, caressed my hair and face, and then he left."

Charles arrives with Joann; he checks the back door, saying, "There's nothing wrong with this door. I don't know how he got in. I'll check the bath and bedrooms."

So Jennifer says to Joann, "So when did you see Charles?"

Joann says, "Well, we came at the same time. That's all."

Jennifer replies, "I see."

Joann asks Jennifer, "What did you mean by that?"

Jennifer says, "I don't mean anything. All I'm saying is it's strange that you both came at the same time. That's all."

Joann replies, "Maybe it's a coincidence. I don't know."

Charles comes out of the bedroom and says, "You see this? This is what I have to put up with, every day, all day: her accusations."

Jennifer replies, "You don't put up with anything because you storm out before anything happens."

Charles yells, "Hey, get the hell off my back, okay?"

Joann replies, "Stop it, both of you stop it."

Charles yells, "I'm leaving."

Jennifer replies, "You might as well because you're useless to me. You show more support for that bitch you are fucking around with."

Charles replies, "Go to hell."

Jennifer replies, "No, you go to hell, you selfish bastard."

So Charles slams the door as he leaves the apartment.

Joann turns to Jennifer and says, "You need to get a hold of yourself."

Jennifer looks at Joann and says, "What the hell do you mean, 'get a hold of myself'? I have been raped. I'm going through this crisis, and my so-called boyfriend is not showing me any kind of support or anything. But still, you're on his side." Joann replies, "I'm not on his side. I'm just saying you shouldn't be arguing right now. Let's deal with this problem first, okay?" Jennifer says, "No, it's not okay. You're going to stand there and tell me that there is nothing going on with him."

Joann says, "All I'm saying is maybe you are pressuring him with your insecurities."

Jennifer replies, "Maybe I have a reason to be insecure, and maybe it's time I start facing up to it."

So Joann says to Jennifer, "I'm going to talk to Charles and see if we can fix this problem, okay?"

Jennifer replies, "Do whatever you want!"

CHAPTER 9

THE NEXT DAY, JENNIFER STOPS AT THE diner and eats her ham and cheese sandwich. She glances at her purse and sees the note the stranger gave her. She opens it and reads it. It says, "What Charles did to you, I will do to him. As for her, you will have to deal with her in your own way. Go to this address tomorrow morning, and you should have some answers about why this is happening to you and me. Like I said, we both deserve each other's love." So as she sips her coffee, she looks around her both ways to see if she's being watched, but she sees nothing.

Meanwhile, Charles is walking to the apartment. Little does he know he's being watched, like a lion watching a gazelle. Before he can step on the first step, the stranger approaches him and says, "Hey." When Charles looks around, the stranger beats the crap out of him, then gets word to Jennifer that Charles is in the hospital.

RAMONE

When Jennifer arrives at the hospital, Joan is there by Charles's side. Jennifer walks into the room and says, "What happened?"

Charles says, "What do you think happened? I was attacked by someone you know." Jennifer replies, "What the hell are you talking about? I don't know anybody who would do this."

Joann says to Jennifer, "Charles believes you sent someone after him."

Jennifer says, "Why would I do that?"

Charles replies, "Because he told me, 'Don't ever touch her again,' and he was talking about you, you fucking bitch."

Joann says to Jennifer, "I know Charles may seem a little rough sometimes, but did you have to send someone after him?"

Jennifer replies, "What part of 'I didn't send anyone after him' did you not understand?"

Then Joann asks, "Why would someone do this to him, and why would they tell him not to touch you anymore? I mean, it just doesn't make sense."

Jennifer replies, "I don't know, gotdammit. Ask Charles!"

Charles says to Jennifer, "There is someone here to see you, Ms. Settle the Score."

The lieutenant enters the room and says, "Miss Day, may I have a few words with you outside?"

Charles says to Jennifer, "Let's see you act innocent and get yourself out of this one."

Jennifer yells, "Fuck the both of you. I didn't do any of this."

Joann replies, "Maybe you'd better go because you are upsetting Charles."

Jennifer replies, "Look at the time, and I'll show you how fast I can get the hell out of here, away from the both of you."

Jennifer exits the room and follows Lt. Bronson out into the hall and into the waiting area. Lt. Bronson asks, "So do you want to tell me what's going on?"

Jennifer replies, "I don't know what's going on! What do you want me to say?"

Lt. Bronson replies, "Did the man who raped you beat up your boyfriend?"

Jennifer then pulls out the note that the stranger gave her and gives it to Lt. Bronson. As Lt. Bronson reads the note, Jennifer explains to him what happened the night she and Charles were arguing.

The lieutenant asks her, "Do you have any idea who this guy could be?"

Jennifer replies, "No, and I don't know if this is the same guy who raped me."

RAMONE

Lt. Bronson says, "Okay, I withdraw the question." He asks, "How often does he contact you?"

Jennifer replies, "I don't know, off and on, I guess, but he seems concerned whenever he contacts me. It's weird and confusing. Something happened to me, and it was different."

The lieutenant replies, "So in other words, he is like your ideal husband who calls to make sure you're alright after any incident occurs?"

Jennifer replies, "You can call it that, yes."

The lieutenant asks, "When was the last contact?"

Jennifer becomes defensive and says, "Am I on trial here?"

Lt. Bronson replies, "No, I just want to get to the bottom of this situation so I can provide answers for you and your friends."

Jennifer says to the lieutenant, "Well, you're looking at me and asking me these questions like I'm a suspect."

The lieutenant has a puzzled look on his face and asks her, "Are you?"

Jennifer replies, "According to those two assholes in there, I am. But you are the expert, so you tell me."

DECISIONS OF THE HEART

The lieutenant pauses and then looks at Jennifer and says, "We'll get to that later, but here's a question for you: Do you think you can get him to meet you somewhere?"

Jennifer asks, "Why?"

The lieutenant replies, "I would like to put you in an apartment under surveillance so we can catch this guy. Are you up to it?"

Jennifer replies, "And if I don't?"

The lieutenant replies, "Then we are back to step one."

Jennifer replies, "Which is?"

The lieutenant says to Jennifer, "You being a possible suspect."

Jennifer looks at the lieutenant with a surprised look on her face as if he told her what color was her underwear.

CHAPTER 10

JENNIFER SITS DOWN THEN HOLDS HER FACE with her elbows against her knees and becomes silent. The lieutenant asks her, "You want us to catch this guy, don't you?"

Jennifer replies, "Yes, yes I do!"

The lieutenant replies, "The next time he contacts you, tell him—I mean really convince him—you want to see him. And if he agrees, you call me right away. Don't do this without me. Do you understand?"

Jennifer keeps her head down and replies, "Yes." The lieutenant tells her to go home. He'll keep in touch with her and then goes back into the room with Charles and Joann.

The lieutenant enters the room and is surprised when he sees Joann and Charles holding hands, and then Joann kisses Charles softly on the lips. When they notice the lieutenant is present, they separate themselves, and Joann sits in the chair.

The lieutenant pauses. Charles then asks, "Are you going to arrest her or not?"

The lieutenant replies, "Well, she is going to cooperate, so maybe we can catch this guy." Charles replies, "If you are going to arrest anyone, it should be her. She had her boyfriend do this to me."

The lieutenant replies, "Well, that's your word against hers, and she said she knows nothing. So if we work with her this way, maybe we can catch him."

CHAPTER 11

THE LIEUTENANT LOOKS OVER AT JOANN AND says to Charles, "I thought she was your girlfriend?" The lieutenant stares at Joann straight into her eyes when he asks Charles that question. Joann cannot look the lieutenant in the face.

Charles replies, "Well, you thought wrong."

The lieutenant replies, "So she is not your girlfriend?" and he looks back at Charles.

Charles replies, "Would my girlfriend have some guy beat the crap out of me? Besides, I and Jennifer broke up a long time ago."

The lieutenant asks, "How long ago?"

Charles says, "I don't know, maybe two months ago."

The lieutenant says, "If it's been that long, why are your belongings still in her apartment?"

Before Charles can answer, Joann steps into the interrogation and says, "Charles, don't say anymore.

These are trick questions. He already knows your things are over there, so why is he asking?"

The lieutenant looks at both and says, "Thank you. I'll be in touch," and he leaves.

The doctor enters the room and says, "Well, you've got a couple of bruises and a fractured finger. I'll prescribe you some pain pills, and you can go home."

Charles and Joann say, "Thank you."

CHAPTER 12

The lieutenant finally makes it home and makes himself a ham and cheese sandwich with lots of mayonnaise while drinking a beer. He sits on the couch to watch some TV and then notices a letter sticking out of his coat pocket.

He opens it up, and it is the note Jennifer gave him, which she got from the stranger. He is particularly interested in the part where it says to go to this address in the morning. Then he looks up and goes, "Hmmmm." He continues drinking his beer and then says to himself, "How nice, an invitation."

So the next day, the lieutenant heads over to the address on the letter which Jennifer gave him. When he arrives, he sits in the car for a few minutes because he has no idea whose address this is. So he is very cautious while getting out of his car. He walks slowly up the stairs, looking both ways and then he knocks on the door.

When the door opens, the lieutenant gets a big surprise: the person answering the door is Charles. He is wearing boxers and nothing else. Charles has a look on his face after seeing the lieutenant as if he just broke his mother's vase, a look of pure guilt.

Then a soft voice in the background says, "Who is it, honey?"

So the lieutenant asks Charles, "May I come in and have a few words with you?"

Charles says to the lieutenant, "Do you have a search warrant?"

The lieutenant replies, "Usually, people say that when they have something to hide. But if it makes you happy, I can go get one and be right back. Or you can save me the trip because either way it goes, I'm going to get to the bottom of this. Now can I come in?" says the lieutenant. Charles steps to the side and lets the lieutenant in. The lieutenant tells Charles to call his companion into the living room.

So Charles calls out, "Can you come in here?"

The woman replies, "I'm naked."

Charles says to the woman, "Put something on and come out here!" So the woman grabs one of Charles's shirts and enters the living room.

As she enters, she walks toward Charles, strokes his face softly, and says, "What's wrong?" Charles turns his head away slowly and then puts his hands on his hips.

When the woman looks toward the position to which Charles turned his head, she is shocked to find herself looking at the lieutenant. The lieutenant isn't shocked at all because he has a gut feeling something is going on between the two.

The lieutenant looks at both of them back and forth and says, "Why am I not surprised?"

Joann replies, "What do you want, Lieutenant?"

The lieutenant says, "I want to find out what's going on."

Joann replies, "This is our personal life. You have no business interfering."

The lieutenant replies, "Well, you are wrong about that because you see, I'm investigating a crime, so as of now, this is my business."

Then he looks at Charles and says, "How long have you and Joann been fooling around behind Jennifer's back?"

Charles pauses and says, "About two months."

The lieutenant then asks, "Do you have any idea who beat you up?"

Charles says, "No, I don't, Lieutenant."

The lieutenant then asks, "Did you have those injuries self-inflicted so you could blame Jennifer and have her arrested so she will be out of your way?"

Charles replies, "Hey, I was attacked, and it was by someone she knew. I didn't do this to myself, okay?"

Joann replies, "Why are you making these accusations against us? We both love Jennifer very much!"

The lieutenant replies, "Basically, until I found out you are screwing your best friend's man and coworker's boyfriend." And then the lieutenant says to Charles, "Let me ask you one more question."

Charles says, "What is that?"

The lieutenant says, "Do you love Jennifer?"

Charles says, "I don't know anymore."

The lieutenant says, "Let me help you out on that. First, you hit her and treat her like garbage, and then you start sleeping with her best friend and coworker. Then she gets raped and abducted, and she gets no kind of support from you or Ms. District Attorney over there. And this is when she needs you the most. And all you can give her is grief, animosity, and attitude. So let me answer that question for you: no, no you don't love her. When you know you don't love someone, let them go. Don't play with their hearts. Just let go. Better now than later. This way, she will have time to get you out of her system."

The lieutenant then turns to Joann and says, "Now let me ask you something. How long have you been friends with Jennifer?"

Joann replies, "I don't have to answer any of your questions without a lawyer, so if I'm not arrested, then arrest me, and then you can interrogate me down at the precinct."

The lieutenant pauses at Joann and then says, "You know, Jennifer talks very highly of you. So I'm sure you and her have been friends for years, and you betrayed years of friendship for two months of sex, and you call yourself her friend? You don't have to worry. I'm not going to mention any of this to Jennifer. It's not relevant to her case, but you will have to live with the guilt of betraying her." Turning to Charles, he says, "Speaking of the case, I'm sure you might want to drop this case that you have against Jennifer, accusing her of having you beat up, am I right, Mr. Charles?"

Charles replies, "Yes, it's over between me and her, so therefore you're not needed here anymore. Is that what you want to hear?"

DECISIONS OF THE HEART

The lieutenant replies, "I want to hear whatever you got to say to me. So you people have a nice, terrible, awful, betraying life."

Then the lieutenant leaves and, before he leaves, he says, "I'm needed by someone who really deserves my help. I'll see ya." Then he leaves.

CHAPTER 13

As the lieutenant is driving, a call comes over the police radio. It says, "We got a call from a Jennifer Day, requesting that Lt. Bronson come to her address."

Then Lt. Bronson replies, "This is Lt. Bronson, and I'm en route, 10-4."

The lieutenant arrives at Jennifer's apartment, and Jennifer greets him at the door and says, "Will you guys be around when he contacts me?"

The lieutenant says, "We will be right outside. He could be watching us. It's not smart to be inside your apartment right now." So Jennifer smiles and says, "Okay, as long as you'll be watching."

"We will be," the lieutenant replies, and they go outside, park a few houses down, and wait.

So Jennifer waits patiently in front of her computer, and then the phone rings. Jennifer answers, "Hello."

On the other end is Joann. Joann says, "How are you?"

Jennifer says, "I'm okay, and you?"

Joann replies, "I feel like shit. I didn't mean any of those bad things I said or thought about you. I'm very sorry." And then Joann starts to cry and says, "Please forgive me. I'm sorry for what I have done."

Jennifer replies, "What are you talking about?"

Joann says, "Did you talk to Lt. Bronson?"

Jennifer replies, "Yes."

Joann says, "What did he say?"

Jennifer says, "He said he wants to catch the guy. That's all. So what are you talking about?" Joann says, "I'm just trying to tell you how bad I felt when we were arguing, and I don't want to argue anymore. I miss my best friend."

Jennifer replies, "I miss you too, and I love you."

Joann replies, "I love you too."

Joann says, "Do you want me to come over?"

Jennifer replies, "Yes, but not right now. I have Lt. Bronson outside in the car, waiting for the stranger to contact me. But I do want you to come over later, okay?"

Joann replies, "Okay, you be careful."

Jennifer says, "I will talk to you later, and I'm glad you called."

Joann replies, "Me too. Bye. Bye."

Joann hangs up the phone and just sits in one position, holding her head down. Charles says to her, "What's wrong?"

Joann replies, "Everything, everything is wrong."

Charles asks, "Did he tell her?"

Joann says, "No, no he didn't."

Charles says, "So what's your problem then?"

Joann replies, "I feel really bad about Jennifer. What we are doing is wrong. I have known Jennifer since we were kids. How can we do this to her?"

Charles says, "Well, you are looking at me like I did something wrong." Joann says, "We both did. I thought this was what I wanted, but after talking to Jennifer just now, I realize she needs me, and her friendship means everything to me."

Charles says, "I didn't make you do anything you didn't want to do."

Joann replies, "I'm not blaming anybody. What happened has happened. I want to make it right with her."

Charles says, "And how are you supposed to do that?"

Joann replies, "I'm going to tell her and ask for her forgiveness."

DECISIONS OF THE HEART

Charles replies, "Are you out of your fucking mind? She's not going to forgive you. She's going to hate us both."

Joann starts crying and says, "I can't live like this anymore. I can't keep betraying her like she means nothing to me when the truth of the matter is, she does. We grew up together. Our moms grew up together."

While Joann is expressing her feelings, Charles is in the background saying, "Oh fuck. I can't believe this shit." Then Charles replies, "You're listening to the lieutenant. Snap your ass out of this guilt thing you are on!"

Joann replies, "No! I can't undo what has been done, but I can do the right thing by confessing to her, and it will be up to her to forgive me."

Then Charles says, "And what am I supposed to do while you are spilling your guts out to her? What are you telling me? That it's over between us? You have some bad vibes, and now you want to end what we got."

Joann replies, "We don't have anything! All we have is a lie and betrayal. We both betrayed someone who meant a lot to us."

Then Charles responds by saying, "No, she meant a lot to you."

RAMONE

Joann pauses and looks at Charles, then says, "Can you honestly look at me with a straight face and say you don't love Jennifer or care for her at all?"

Charles looks at Joann with a straight face and says, "Two months ago, if you would have asked me that question, I would have said yes, I love her, but now I love you."

He walks up to Joann, hugs her, and strokes her face softly while looking into her eyes, saying, "I love you."

Joann starts crying, looking right back into Charles's eyes, and says, "I'm sorry, Charles, but I can't do this anymore. My friend needs me."

Charles says, "I need you too! Who's more important, me or her?"

Joann replies, "She's important. I was wrong for letting us go this far."

Charles replies, "If you can look me in the eye and tell me you don't love me, I will walk out of here, and you will never see or hear from me again. Now tell me, do you love me or not?"

Joann replies, "I have no right to love someone who doesn't belong to me."

Charles replies, "Shut the fuck up and answer the gotdamn question!"

Joann replies, "Why can't you understand, Charles? She needs me. She needs me."

Charles replies, "Fuck this shit, I'm out of here," and he starts packing his bag.

As he is walking out the door, Joann calls to him, "Charles!"

Charles replies, "What the fuck is it now?"

Joann replies, "A cold heart might as well be dead." Charles looks at her and says, "Did the lieutenant tell you that one too!"

Joann replies, "No, he didn't. But my heart did, and no matter what the outcome of this situation, I'm going to cleanse my soul and tell Jennifer the truth. So wherever you are going, remember this: she did not ask for any of this. We owe it to her to tell the truth, and I was hoping you would come with me when I tell her."

Charles replies, "You and Jennifer have a nice life. I'm out of here," and then Charles is gone.

Meanwhile, back at Jennifer's apartment, the phone rings. Jennifer answers with a sweet voice, "Hello."

The stranger replies, "It's me."

Jennifer takes a deep breath and says, "I was waiting for you to call."

The stranger says, "Were you?"

RAMONE

Jennifer says, "Yes, I wanted to talk to you."

The stranger says, "What about?" Jennifer replies, "Well, I don't really know you, or what you're like, or your name, not that it would matter. I just wanted to know a little about you."

The stranger replies, "Well, how badly would you like to see me?"

Jennifer replies, "As soon as possible. There are questions that I need to ask you, which I just don't understand."

The stranger asks, "Which is?"

Jennifer replies, "First of all, you beat up my boyfriend, Charles, really badly, then you raped me, and now you're following me around, protecting me, after what you have done. I just don't understand why!"

The stranger replies, "It's simple. I kicked his ass because he was a jerk, and he didn't appreciate the love you had for him."

Jennifer replies, "Okay. Go on."

The stranger replies, "I didn't rape you. I made love to you. You see, you're like an angel, an angel without wings, and I believe God brought us into each other's lives because we need each other like we need the air to breathe. God chose me to be with you because he heard your cry for help, so he sent

DECISIONS OF THE HEART

me because he knows my heart is filled with love, respect, and honor for you. I love you, Jennifer. I love you more than any man could ever know. You would never have to worry about me messing around, breaking your heart, or bringing you down, and it wouldn't be just a sex thing, okay? I am in love with you. I will always be there for you. You will never have to wonder if I love you because every day that goes by, my love for you will grow stronger and stronger. You will never have to ask any of your friends or coworkers if I love you, because you will know. You will know what's at the other end of the rainbow because I will show you. You will never lay in bed in need of attention, comfort, or love and affection. All your sexual needs will be fulfilled. If you ever need me for anything, all you have to do is call me, wait five seconds, and then look over your shoulder, and there I'll be."

While the stranger is revealing his emotions to Jennifer, she cries silently, her heart racing with joy, for this is the man she's been praying for all her life. Now she's confused; she doesn't know what to say or do, so she continues to listen. The stranger finishes by saying, "Jennifer, I love you, and I need you to love me. I don't want to hide from you anymore. So if you truly want to see me, you can because I don't

RAMONE

care what happens to me anymore. I'm willing to put my heart into your hands because I love you enough to trust you. I will meet with you and reveal my identity. I don't care if you have the cops waiting for me or not because the only thing that matters to me is you. Without you, there's no purpose. So if you really want to meet with me, just say when, where, and what time, and I'll be there." Jennifer is quiet; she puts her hand across her chest as if she can't breathe. The whole time the stranger is revealing his emotions to Jennifer, the radio plays softly a song titled "We Both Deserve Each Other's Love."

So Jennifer, with tears in her eyes, doesn't reply to the stranger. The stranger asks, "Jennifer, are you still there?"

Jennifer replies, "Yes, I'm still here. And yes, I would like to meet you."

The stranger says, "Okay, where would you like to meet me?"

Jennifer says, "At the diner, where I usually order my takeout food. So if you have been following me, I'm sure you know which diner it is and what kind of car I have, right?"

The stranger replies, "Yes, but you don't have a car. You have a truck."

Jennifer replies, "You're very observant."

The stranger replies, "Well, I call it like I see it."

Then Jennifer says to the stranger, "Could you meet me at…" and before she can finish her sentence, the officer, who is taping the conversation, holds up two fingers and one hand, indicating for her to say 7:00 p.m. So Jennifer continues, "Make it 7:00 p.m., okay?"

The stranger replies, "Yes, anything for you. I'll see you later."

And before the stranger can hang up, Jennifer shouts, "Wait! If you don't see my truck, keep going. Don't wait, okay?"

The stranger replies, "I don't understand, but whatever you say."

As Jennifer hangs up the phone, the officer who is trying to trace the call says, "He's on a cell phone, and the number won't be traced. I believe he's scrambling the system." The lieutenant enters the apartment and walks straight over to Jennifer, saying with an angry voice, "What the hell was that about?"

Jennifer replies, "What do you mean?"

The lieutenant pauses for a minute or two and says, "Let's keep in mind that this is the guy who raped you, okay?"

Jennifer shouts, "I know that! He's meeting me, okay?"

RAMONE

The lieutenant looks at her with a suspicious look and says very calmly, "Yes, he is." The lieutenant says to Jennifer, "He's the bad guy, okay?"

Jennifer replies, "The way things have been going in my life, it's hard to tell who's the bad guy!"

The lieutenant replies, "You're so right. 100 percent."

Jennifer replies, "What do you mean by that? Are you trying to tell me something?"

The lieutenant pauses and changes his suspicious look to a charitable look. He says, "Just keep your guard up, and a shield over your heart."

Jennifer replies, "Okay, are you going to tell me, or are you going to continue to speak in tongues?"

The lieutenant says, "Listen, let's just go over our game plan and bring this man to justice, okay? Now there will be two unmarked cars following you, and I will be at the diner on the south side of the street, in a white van. We will have a table reserved for you and him. You will sit at that table and wait for him to arrive. We will have two couples sitting on each side of you having dinner. These couples are police officers. When you get him to confess to the rape, we will move in. You understand?"

Jennifer replies, "Yes, but you still haven't answered my question."

DECISIONS OF THE HEART

The lieutenant replies, "I would like to, Ms. Day, but that question is not relevant to this case."

Jennifer replies, "Then can you tell me as a friend and not as a lieutenant?"

The lieutenant replies, "If this operation goes as well as we plan, I will tell you all that I know, okay?"

Jennifer replies, "Yeah, sure."

The lieutenant says to Jennifer, "Now get some sleep. We have a big day tomorrow."

They all leave, and Jennifer gets ready for bed. There is a knock on the door. It's Joann, Bob, and Johnny. Jennifer is very happy to see them. They are all hugging her as if they haven't seen her in years. And then Jennifer says, "So to whom do I owe this surprise visit?"

Joann replies, "Well, we're giving you something we should have given you a long time ago: support."

Jennifer is very happy. Then Bob says, "Hey, let's order some pizza to go with all this beer we got?"

Johnny says, "For once, you're using your head because I'm hungry as hell."

So Joann says, "That's a good idea. Why don't you guys make the call? The phone is in the other room."

As Bob and Johnny go to the other room, Bob yells, "Anchovies."

Jennifer yells back, "Put everything on it."

Then Johnny replies, "But hold the anchovies."

And then Bob says, "No way. You eat anchovies or die!"

Joann asks Jennifer, "Are you alright?"

Jennifer replies, "Yes, well, no."

Joann asks, "What's wrong?" Jennifer explains to Joann about the lieutenant's plan to capture the stranger. Joann says, "That's great. We're finally going to catch this creep."

Jennifer replies, "I'm confused."

Joann asks, "About what?"

Jennifer replies, "Well, he revealed so much to me things I never knew."

Joann replies, "What things? What the hell are you talking about?"

Jennifer says, "Well, he told me all his reasons why he did what he did."

And before Jennifer can complete her sentence, Joann cuts her off and says, "Wait a minute, are we talking about the same guy who raped you?"

Jennifer replies, "I know it sounds crazy, but I almost felt him," as Jennifer touches her chest softly, "right here, you know? I can relate to what he was saying because he actually has been through the same thing I have. I mean, he didn't actually say it, but I can tell."

Joann replies, "Jennifer, please, get a grip on yourself, okay? This man raped you, abducted you, tied you up with duct tape, and had his way with you."

Jennifer replies, "He did no more than what boyfriends and husbands are doing to their girlfriends and wives today, so why should I alienate him for that?"

Joann replies, "Because you didn't give it to him. He took it. Doesn't that make you feel bad, knowing that he tore your panties off and ignored you screaming now? Do you honestly think that makes it alright?"

Jennifer replies, "I know it was wrong the way that it happened, but I believe he's sorry for the way it did happen. I mean, maybe he was afraid to approach me. Maybe he thought that I would reject him."

Joann replies, "Jennifer, reality check, okay? He hospitalized you. You talked to the police, a lieutenant, may I add, and the rape advocate. Have you forgotten?"

Jennifer replies, "Look, I know all that! You just don't understand, no matter how I explain it to you. I'm telling you, I felt him."

RAMONE

So Joann asks Jennifer, "What's your next move?"

Jennifer says, "He's meeting with me at the diner."

"Are you crazy? You don't know what he might do. You're not meeting with him."

Jennifer replies, "Don't worry. The lieutenant and the police will be there to try and catch him, but I'm not sure if I want to turn him in."

"Hey, you do it. You meet with him so we can find out if he's done this to anybody else, okay?"

"I don't think he did this to anybody."

Joann replies, "And what makes you so sure of that?"

"Because he said he loves me."

Joann says, "Anybody could say that, but that doesn't mean they do. Maybe he wants to hurt you."

Jennifer yells, "No, he doesn't want to hurt me."

Joann asks, "How do you know that?"

"Because he's been protecting me. Everywhere I go, he's there watching over me."

"How does he watch over you?"

"Well, I have been attacked more than once. After I left the hospital, I was attacked in the parking lot."

Joann, with a worried look on her face, asks, "Did you call the police?"

Jennifer says, "No."

Joann asks, "Why not?"

Jennifer replies, "Because I didn't have to. The stranger took care of it."

"What did he do?"

"Well, I was walking to my truck, and I noticed a shadow behind me and all of a sudden, I was pushed against the truck really hard. Then he pushed me down to the ground and took my purse and ran off. Next thing I know, I'm on the ground screaming, 'Fuck! Not again.'"

Joann asks, "Oh my god, did he hurt you?"

Jennifer replies, "Well, I just bumped my chin against the window. Nothing serious."

"So how did the stranger help you?"

"Well, when I got home, as I was walking up the stairs, I heard the ambulance coming. They stopped two houses down from me, and they were putting a man in the ambulance. It just so happens to be the same man who attacked me and took my purse."

"Well, maybe he tried to take someone else's purse and got what he deserved, but what does this have to do with you?"

RAMONE

Jennifer replies, "Well, as I was reaching for the doorknob, I noticed my purse was hanging from it with a note attached to it."

Joann asks, "What did the note say?"

Jennifer says the note said, "'There are times I don't think of you, and those are the times I think about us. Here's your purse. That guy will never bother you again.' And then I called the hospital to find out if anybody was brought in recently, and they told me there was a guy in there with a busted eye, fingers broken, all of them, also cracked ribs."

Joann replies, "This sounds serious. Maybe you should have told the police about this."

Jennifer replies, "I didn't tell anyone because he was protecting me."

And then a knock on the door interrupts them. Joann answers, "Who is it?"

The voice on the other side says, "Pizza man!" Bob and Johnny run toward the door, screaming, "Get out of the way!" like a couple of kids.

Jennifer and Joann were laughing at Bob and Johnny's childhood effort running after the pizza man.

Jennifer says to Joann, "Can we talk about this later because I'm kind of hungry too?"

Joann says, "On one condition."

Jennifer replies, "And what's that?"

Joann says, "You meet with the lieutenant in the morning."

Jennifer replies, "Okay, I'm too tired to argue with you."

"Okay, let's eat."

So they play their music and eat their pizza through the night, listening to a song called "Murder She Wrote."

The next day, Jennifer awakens to a messy apartment. Beer cans and pizza are everywhere on the floor. She also awakes with a hangover from drinking too much the night before. The phone rings. Jennifer answers, "Hello?"

The caller replies, "Good morning. This is Lt. Bronson."

"Good morning. Is it 7:00 p.m. already?"

The lieutenant says, "No, I'm just giving you a reminder of our appointment today."

"Oh, I have a hangover."

"What happened? Did you go and party last night? Because if you did, that's a good thing. You need to get out and clear your mind."

"Actually, my friends came over to show me some support for my incident."

The lieutenant pauses for a few seconds, then says, "Including Joann?"

Jennifer yells, "Yes, including Joann. She's my best friend! What's going on with you and Joann?"

The lieutenant answers, "Nothing. I was just wondering if you two made up, that's all. Nothing to get all worked up about."

Jennifer says, "Yes, we made up."

"Good. Good for you."

"Look, I don't mean to be rude, but I got a lot of cleaning to do."

As she starts to yawn, the lieutenant says, "Okay, I'll see you at 7:00 p.m. tonight. Okay, bye."

So Jennifer hangs up the phone and begins to clean up. As she is cleaning, one of her favorite songs comes on the radio, the name of which is "100% Pure Love" by Crystal Waters. She starts dancing and singing while vacuuming the floor, just enjoying herself.

CHAPTER 14
The Chase

LATER, AROUND 6:30 P.M., JENNIFER SITS ON the couch with her legs crossed over the other and her arms crossed. She looks at the clock, waiting for Lt. Bronson to arrive. As she waits, she starts to have flashbacks about what happened to her. She thinks of everything about the stranger, all that he's done to her, from the rape to putting Charles in the hospital. She thinks about the lieutenant wanting to catch him and Joann encouraging her to help the lieutenant in every way, all the things the stranger had told her about how he feels for her, which is making her very confused about everything. She's now debating on what she should do, and then the doorbell rings, snapping her right out of her deep thoughts. She answers the door, and it's the lieutenant. She looks at him and then at her watch and says, "You're right on time."

The lieutenant says, "Let's go get him."

So they get maybe a block away from the restaurant where Jennifer and the stranger are supposed to meet, and they go over a few details. The lieutenant says, "Are you ready?"

Jennifer replies, "Yes," in an unsure way.

"Look, we can't do this without you. So either you're with this or not."

"Yes."

"Ok, I know you can do this. We are right behind you, so go on."

Jennifer drives off, looking very nervous and frightened as if she's going underwater. The officer says to the lieutenant, "We're gonna get this piece of shit, right?"

The lieutenant replies very loudly and slowly, "If we get him, we're going to have to get him on our own without her." The officer looks at him, and he is puzzled.

Jennifer gets closer and closer to the restaurant. She pulls in front of it and pauses. She looks inside the window of the restaurant and sees plenty of people sitting down, eating, and then she starts a silent cry and pulls off.

DECISIONS OF THE HEART

The officer says, "Fuck, what the hell is she doing?" The lieutenant just sits there, saying nothing, and stares at her as she drives away. Meanwhile, inside the restaurant, the stranger notices Jennifer driving away. He kindly gets up from his table and walks away.

As the stranger drives away, the lieutenant notices the black van. He remembers Jennifer told him she was put in a black van. The lieutenant yells, "It's him, it's him!"

Another officer yells, "Where?"

The lieutenant says, "The black van. Let's go, let's go!"

All the officers jump into their cars and begin the chase. The stranger looks into his rearview mirror and sees what's going on, so he puts the pedal to the metal. There are many close calls because the chase is very intense; they weave through cars, traffic, pedestrians, and alleys as if they are the only ones on the streets. The lieutenant is on his tail, then he yells, "We got him, we got him!"

Suddenly a fifty-foot truck is backing out with a guide giving him the clearance to do so. The stranger narrowly misses the guide but gets by. The lieutenant and his officers are delayed by the big truck. The lieutenant gets out of his car and yells, "Get that damn thing out of the way!" So the guide tells the truck driver to pull forward. As the driver attempts to pull forward, the truck stalls. The lieutenant and officers are yelling and screaming at the driver, "Move this piece of shit right fucking now!" The driver finally gets the truck started and pulls forward, and the lieutenant and officers speed by, but it's too late. The stranger is gone as if he was never there. The lieutenant gets out of his car with a very angry look on his face as if someone stole his favorite squad car. He's looking around and is very pissed off.

One of the officers says, "Fuck! We lost him."

The lieutenant stares off in the direction in which the stranger was traveling and says in a whispering voice, "He's gonna slip, and when he does, I'm gonna bust his ass."

Jennifer pulls in front of her apartment with tears in her eyes and runs up the stairs. She goes into her living room, sits on the couch, and says, "What the fuck is wrong with me?" She has so much frustration in her voice. Then the phone rings. She answers the phone, assuming it's the lieutenant. She's frustrated, angry, and confused, so she yells, "I'm sorry, Lieutenant, but I can't have you and everybody else pressuring me about this!"

Then a soft, strong voice says on the phone, "Hello, Jennifer."

Jennifer pauses and yet feels relieved at the same time. The stranger says, "You could've turned me in. Why didn't you?"

Jennifer replies with a soft, crackling voice, "I don't know."

The stranger says, "Maybe you didn't turn me in because you know in your heart that I love you, and maybe you love me too."

Jennifer replies, "Why are you doing this to me? I had a good life before you came along."

The stranger says, "Did you? Did you really have a good life before I came along? I'm the only one out there who cares about you. No one out there loves you more than me."

Jennifer says, "I don't know you, and you don't know me. How can you say this stuff to me?"

The stranger replies, "You should know by now how I feel about you and how you feel about me. I told you what happened, happened for a reason. We deserve each other, and you know it. Why the hell are you fighting what's meant to be?"

Jennifer says very softly, "Please leave me alone."

"If I leave you alone, you will have nothing. Nothing at all. I'm the one who loves you."

And the stranger hangs up.

CHAPTER 15

There's a knock at the door. Jennifer answers, "Who is it?"

The person says, "It's Joann."

Jennifer opens the door, and Joann storms in. She says, "I can't believe you didn't go through with it. What's the matter with you?"

Jennifer says, "Look, I don't want to talk about it, okay?"

Joann says, "What do you mean you don't want to talk about it? They could've caught him."

Jennifer replies, "Maybe I don't want them to catch him."

Joann looks very shocked and says, "What are you saying? That you like this guy? That you like what he did to you?"

Jennifer replies, "What did he do to me?"

Joann says, "He went to the fucking toilet on you!"

Jennifer says, "No, that's what your loving, sneaking-in-the-back-door Charles did to me."

Joann replies, "I don't care what you say. You don't know this guy."

Jennifer said, "I know one thing for sure. He cares about me more than your precious friend Charles ever did."

Joann says, "Do you hear what you're saying? Do you actually care about this guy who fucking raped you?"

Jennifer says, "Maybe he saved me from a relationship that was going nowhere, or maybe I am just losing my fucking mind. But I think I may have feelings for him."

Then Jennifer holds her head down while sitting on the couch with her knees together and her feet apart. Joann replies, "Jennifer, are you sure you feel this way about him, considering the fact that he abducted, raped, and held you hostage against your own will?"

Jennifer holds her head up high, with a sad look on her face, and says, "I don't know anymore."

Joann looks at Jennifer and pauses. It's very quiet now.

CHAPTER 16
The Confession

Joann tells Jennifer, "I have something to tell you."

Jennifer asks, "What?" Joann starts to cry. Jennifer says, "Joann, what's wrong? Whatever it is, you can tell me."

Joann says, "I want you to know that I am very sorry for what I'm going to say, and I love you so much. I never meant for this to happen, and I'm asking for your forgiveness."

Jennifer yells, "What! What is it, Joann?" Joann looks at Jennifer straight in the eyes, and then Jennifer's mouth drops as if she already knows what Joann is about to tell her. Jennifer says, "Oh my God."

Joann says, "Please forgive me, Jennifer."

Jennifer replies, "So that's what the lieutenant was talking about. That's how you knew what Charles was going to do to me the next day. I can't fucking believe this shit. You actually had to tell my fucking no-good-ass boyfriend to make love to me? Oh, wait, I mean to go to the fucking toilet on me because that's what he did."

While Jennifer walks away, Joann replies, "But I broke it off with him. You have to believe me! I told him you mean more to me than he does."

Jennifer says, "Oh yeah! That's why you were fucking him, right?"

Joann says, "No, no, that's not it!"

Jennifer replies, "You're nothing but a cheap slut."

Joann says, "I'm sorry. What do you want me to do? It happened."

Jennifer says, "You're supposed to be my best friend. How can you do this to me and then say it just happened?"

Joann says, "It did, and I am sorry I let this happen. Please forgive me."

Jennifer says, "If you were any kind of best friend of mine, you wouldn't let this happen."

Joann says, "Jennifer, is there anything I could do to make this up to you?"

"Yes, there is. You can start by getting your filthy ass out of my house, you fucking bitch."

Joann walks out very slowly as if she were a ten-year-old girl leaving her favorite doll behind. Jennifer closes the door very gently and starts to cry, leaning forward with her head against the door then she goes to bed.

CHAPTER 17

THE NEXT DAY, JENNIFER CALLS THE LIEUTENANT and says, "Why didn't you tell me what was going on, you fucking bastard?"

The lieutenant replies, "Hey, take it easy!"

Jennifer says, "No, you take it easy!"

Lt says, "That situation was irrelevant to this case. It was personal."

Jennifer replies, "Oh, so it's okay for me to spill my guts out to you and get nothing in return?"

Lt says, "That was a personal matter. I would have been out of place to interfere."

Jennifer says, "Whatever, it's been done now."

The lieutenant says, "So are you going to help us catch this guy or what?"

Jennifer replies, "I'll get back to you on that."

Lt says, "Yeah, I'm sure you will." Then he hangs up.

RAMONE

When Jennifer hangs up, the phone rings. She answers very angrily, "What?"

It's the stranger. He says, "Hi," in a very calm voice, "How are you?"

Jennifer says, "I've been better."

The stranger says, "So I guess you had a talk with Joann?"

Jennifer says, "You sure do know a lot about what's going on with me, don't you?"

The stranger says, "Yes, I do, only with what concerns you. I want you to know that I miss you very much."

Jennifer replies, "I'm not going to fight this anymore. Maybe I'm crazy, but I've been thinking about you too. But the funny thing about that is, aahh, I've never seen you. I don't even know what you look like, what's your favorite color, or what kind of foods you eat."

The stranger says, "Would you like to know these things?"

Jennifer replies, "Yes, yes, I would like to know things about you."

The stranger says, "Okay, let's meet?"

Jennifer says, "Where?"

The stranger says, "At the park." Jennifer says, "Okay, at the park."

The stranger replies, "What time is good for you?"

Jennifer says, "How about 3:00 p.m.?"

The stranger says, "Three o'clock it is."

Jennifer seems kind of excited and can't wait to finally meet her mystery man. But she isn't aware of the plans that Lt. Bronson has in store for her. Sitting in a dark-colored minivan across the street, he listens to every conversation that Jennifer may have on her phone calls. He is preparing himself to catch the stranger, without Jennifer's acknowledgment or consultancy.

A few hours later, Jennifer calls Joann. She was so happy from the last phone call she had with this stranger; she decided to forgive her friend Joann. Now there is no confusion in her life anymore concerning the stranger. She now knows what she wants and wants to share that with Joann. Her life seems to be fulfilled now. Jennifer says, "Hello, Joann."

Then Joann takes a deep breath as if she was underwater, finally releases it, and says, "Oh my God, thank you for calling me. Is everything okay?"

Jennifer says, "Well, I thought about it, and Charles was a lost cause anyway, so maybe you did me a favor."

Joann says, "Never mind that. What's important is we're talking again."

Jennifer says, "I'm going to meet with him."

Joann says, "By yourself? Do you want me to go with you?"

Jennifer says, "No, I think I will be alright."

Joann says, "Well, maybe you should call the lieutenant, you know, just to be on the safe side."

Jennifer says, "I'm going to do this all on my own because, believe it or not, I trust him. And if he wanted to do something to me, he would've already done it by now. I feel really safe knowing that I will be with him. I know you and the lieutenant don't understand, but this is what I want."

Joann says, "I want you to promise me if you have any doubts whatsoever, please turn back, okay?"

Jennifer replies, "Okay, I promise."

So they both say bye to each other and hang up.

CHAPTER 18

As Jennifer drives to the park, one of her favorite songs comes on the radio, "Here We Are" by Gloria Estefan. She arrives at the park and happily walks toward the bench, sitting down with a smile on her face as if she is going on her prom date. Unbeknownst to her, she is being followed by Lt. Bronson and his men. Suddenly, a stranger appears. He walks toward her, and Jennifer smiles at him, asking, "Is it you?"

The stranger looks at her, smiles, and then strikes her across the face. Jennifer starts screaming as he pulls out a gun and yells, "Give me the fucking purse, or I'll kill you, bitch!" Jennifer, terrified, hears the stranger yell again, "Give me the purse, bitch!" He draws his fist back as if he is going to hit her again. Jennifer screams, closes her eyes, and tilts her head sideways to prepare for the impact of the stranger's fist.

RAMONE

Then a man jumps out of nowhere and grabs the stranger from behind. They roll off Jennifer and begin to fight, exchanging several blows to the head, body, and face. The man who saved Jennifer from harm is winning the fight. The robber then points the gun at the stranger, but the stranger knocks the gun from the robber's hand. As the gun falls to the ground, the robber dives for it and succeeds. While on the ground, he points the gun at the stranger and shoots him in the stomach. The stranger goes down like a ton of bricks. Jennifer screams, "No!"

The robber attempts to run but is apprehended by Lt. Bronson and his officers. The robber is handcuffed and taken away. Lt. Bronson calls for an ambulance on his walkie-talkie and gives first aid to the stranger, asking, "Are you alright?" The stranger doesn't say anything. Lt. Bronson asks, "Who are you? You risked your life for this woman. You did a very brave thing."

Jennifer jumps up, runs toward the stranger, and says, "Are you alright? Thank you, thank you for saving—" Before she can finish, she sees something shocking.

The lieutenant asks, "What's wrong?"

Jennifer just stands there with her mouth wide open, tears running down her face. The ambulance arrives and carries the stranger away.

Before they put him inside the ambulance, Jennifer grabs the stranger by his shirt, yelling, "Why? Why? How could you do this to me?" Lt. Bronson stands behind Jennifer, holding her by her arms. Jennifer yells, "Johnny, you were my friend, how could you? How could you?" She starts crying and runs away.

Lt. Bronson reads Johnny his rights as he is placed under arrest for the rape and abduction of Jennifer Day. Lt. Bronson says to Johnny, "You know what they do to guys who rape women when they go to prison."

He pauses, looks Johnny in the eyes, and says, "I hope you got a cork in it. Take him away."

CHAPTER 19

So Jennifer makes it home. She stands in one spot, looking around her apartment, and then she loses it. She starts throwing things, yelling, screaming, breaking everything she can get her hands on. She grabs a photo of her, Johnny, Bob, and Joann. She attempts to throw it, but she can't. She falls to her knees, looks at the photo, and starts to cry, crying herself to sleep.

So the next day, Jennifer gets a call; it's the lieutenant. He calls to tell her which hospital Johnny is in and also to come and sign a complaint. The lieutenant asks, "Do you want to press charges?"

Jennifer replies, "Yes."

The lieutenant says, "I'll see you soon," and then he hangs up.

Joann comes over to see Jennifer and asks, "Are you alright?"

Jennifer says, "Yes, I'm okay."

Joann says, "So what do you want to do?"

Jennifer says, "I have a lot of questions, but I really don't know what I want to do just yet."

Joann says, "Let's go."

Jennifer asks, "Where?"

Joann says, "Let's go see Johnny."

Jennifer just stands there, so Joann grabs her hand and says, "Let's go. You said you have a lot of questions, so let's go." Joann leads Jennifer out the door, and away they went.

When they arrive at the hospital, they notice an officer sitting outside Johnny's room door. Jennifer reveals to the officer who she is, and the officer looks toward the lieutenant to get an okay, which he does. Jennifer and Joann walk into the room and stand by Johnny's bed. Johnny has tubes up his nostrils so he can breathe because of the gunshot. Johnny is very weak but is recovering slowly. His wrist is handcuffed to the bed rails. Jennifer looks at him and says very softly, "Why? Why, Johnny?"

Johnny takes a deep breath and says in a weak voice, "I was tired of hearing how bad Charles was treating you. Your love wasn't good enough for him. All I wanted to do is show you there is someone out there who very much appreciates you, and that's me. I have always loved you. I just didn't know how you would feel about me. I didn't know how you would feel about a Black man being in love with you."

Jennifer replies, "You were my friend. If I had a problem with Black people, I would've never been your friend."

Johnny said, "I'm sorry. I know I've hurt you, but hurting you was the last thing I ever wanted to do."

Jennifer replies, "Why?"

Johnny says, "Because I love you."

Tears fill Jennifer's eyes, and she says, "Damn you," then runs out of the room and out of the hospital, with Joann on her tail. Joann yells Jennifer's name while running after her, but Jennifer doesn't stop running until she gets to the car. They both get in the car and drive away.

While they are driving, Joann asks, "What's wrong?"

Jennifer says, "I don't know what's wrong, but while I was talking to him, I got this weird feeling in my stomach."

Joann says, "Well, maybe you love him too."

Jennifer yells, "I don't! I mean, how could I love someone who raped me? He fucking betrayed me, and for me to go along with this, I have to be out of my fucking mind."

Joann says, "Oh, okay. So what happened to that damn song you were singing to me not too long ago!"

Jennifer says, "I don't know, gotdammit. Just leave me the fuck alone."

Joann says, "No! I won't leave you the fuck alone. You need him, and he needs you. And if you bother to take your head out of your ass, you'll see that I am right."

Jennifer replies, "I don't need anyone."

Joann says, "Yes, you do. It's not like you don't know him or anything, so stop being a stubborn bitch and do yourself a favor and just do it, Jennifer."

Jennifer asks, "Do what?"

Joann says, "Go to him. He did for you what Charles wouldn't have done in your wildest dreams. He risked his life for you. He must really love you to do that. And yes, I know I was against it at first, but even a blind person could see he's right for you, no matter what color he is."

Jennifer looks at Joann with tears in her eyes and asks, "Why are you saying this to me?"

Joann says, "Because you're my friend, and I want to make it up to you by guiding you to your blessings. I love you, Jennifer."

RAMONE

Jennifer pauses, and this song comes on the radio. It's called "We Both Deserve Each Other's Love" by Jeffrey Osborne. Jennifer makes a hard stop at the traffic light, and Joann looks at Jennifer and says, "Go. Go to him."

Jennifer looks at Joann and says, "Fuck you, Joann." Jennifer jumps out of the car, running toward the hospital as if she is running a marathon. While she's running, the song is still playing in her head. The lieutenant and a few of his officers are standing by the front desk as she runs past them and straight to Johnny's room. The officer says to the lieutenant, "Now what is she up to?"

The lieutenant says, "It's over. That's what she's up to. She's in love."

Jennifer gets in the room, breathing heavily. She sits down on the side of Johnny's bed with tears in her eyes and says, "Next time just ask." Then she smiles.

The lieutenant walks in and tells the officers to uncuff him. Jennifer turns her head toward the officer and says, "Yes, uncuff my man."

After they uncuff him, the lieutenant says, "Okay, boys, let's go."

Then Jennifer hugs Johnny and puts her head on his chest, and Johnny hugs her right back.

DECISIONS OF THE HEART

After Johnny is better, Jennifer takes him to her apartment to look after him while he recuperates. With one arm around her and the other on the banister, they go in and close the door behind them. Now Jennifer's life is fulfilled. That's the end of Jennifer Day's story.

*****

This novel ends with another couple. A Black couple walks into an office building. The woman tells her boyfriend to wait for her in the waiting area, but before he goes, she's swearing and yelling at him. She tells him how much of a lesser man he is, making him feel like nothing. So he goes and sits in the waiting room. He happens to look down the hall where his girlfriend is standing and notices she is flirting with one of the employees. He goes back to the waiting area and sits down, holding his head down, sinking into a deep, sad depression.

There is a woman sitting in the waiting area before the Black couple came in. She is an Asian woman, and she watches how the man is disrespected and how awfully he is treated. Then she sees how his girlfriend is flirting with an employee. She stares at the depressed man sitting across her with no expression on her face. The man has his head down, but he doesn't know that a decision of the heart is about to happen to him. The end.

ABOUT THE AUTHOR

Since I was a kid, I have watched movies. Those movies inspired me to be a writer. I would change the scene of a movie in my head while watching it. Watching all kinds of movies is how I got my inspiration.

Printed in the USA
CPSIA information can be obtained
at www.ICGtesting.com
CBHW022202271124
18026CB00041B/636